JUN   2012

OLIVER

Written and illustrated by Judith Rossell

HARPER

An Imprint of HarperCollinsPublishers

Thank you to the
May Gibbs Children's Literature Trust

Oliver
Copyright © 2012 by Judith Rossell
All rights reserved.
Manufactured in China.
No part of this book may be used or reproduced in any manner
whatsoever without written permission except in the case of brief
quotations embodied in critical articles and reviews.
For information address HarperCollins Children's Books, a division of
HarperCollins Publishers, 10 East 53rd Street, New York, NY 10022.
www.harpercollinschildrens.com

Library of Congress Cataloging-in-Publication Data is available.
ISBN 978-0-06-202210-3

Typography by Jeanne L. Hogle & Suzan Choy
12   13   14   15   16   SCP   10   9   8   7   6   5   4   3   2   1
❖
First Edition

For Henry and Matthew
—J.R.

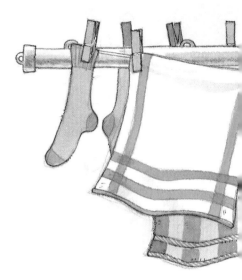

"How do planes stay up in the sky?"
Oliver asked.

Oliver liked finding things out.

"Wings," said his mom with her mouth full of clothespins.

"Wings?"

Oliver found out everything he could about wings.

He already knew about Band-Aids.

"How does the fridge work?" asked Oliver.

"Please shut the door, Oliver. You're letting the cold out," said Mom.

"Could a penguin live in our fridge?" he asked.

"Penguins live in Antarctica," said Mom.

"What if he was on vacation?" asked Oliver.

Mom laughed. "Maybe," she said.

At lunch, Oliver found out more than he wanted to about broccoli.
"Just eat it up, please, Oliver," said Mom. "And don't slurp your milk."

After lunch, Oliver found things out inside

and outside

until Mom said it was time for a bath.
"Do I have to?" asked Oliver.

Oliver jumped into the tub.

"How can I breathe underwater like a fish?" asked Oliver.

"Fish don't splash like that," called Mom. "Fish are very quiet."

Oliver pulled out the plug. "What lives down the drain?" he asked.

"Nothing," said Mom. "Just pipes."

"There's something down there," shouted Oliver. "I can hear it GURGLING."

"Maybe it's a MONSTER. I think it's HUNGRY."

Oliver climbed out of the bathtub and got a banana from the kitchen.

"I'm going to poke it down the drain," he said.

"No, you're not," said Mom firmly.

"You never let me do anything," said Oliver.

"Get dry, get dressed," said Mom. "And how about taking a nap?"

"I'm not tired," said Oliver.

"I am," said Mom. "You do something quiet. Do some drawing."

So Oliver drew a
submarine . . .

and then he built it.
  "I'm going to find out what's
down the drain," he said.

"Did you hear me, Mom? I'm going down the drain.

"And I might not come back."

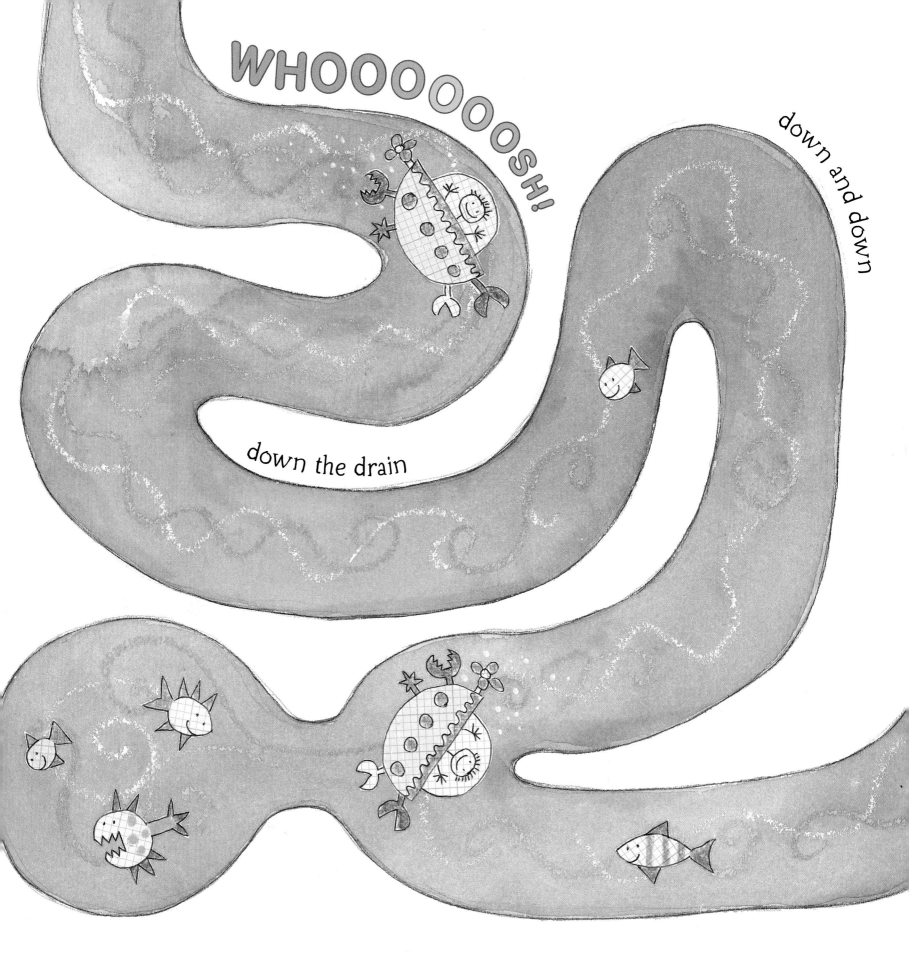

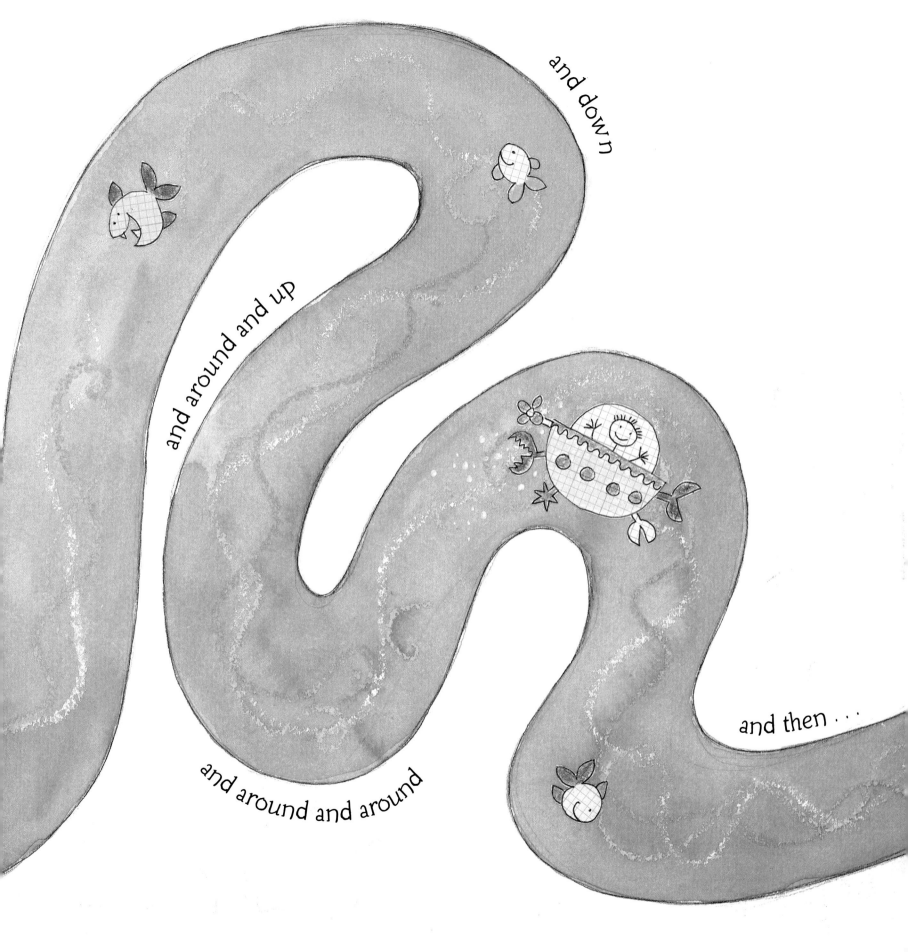

and down

and around and up

and around and around

and then . . .

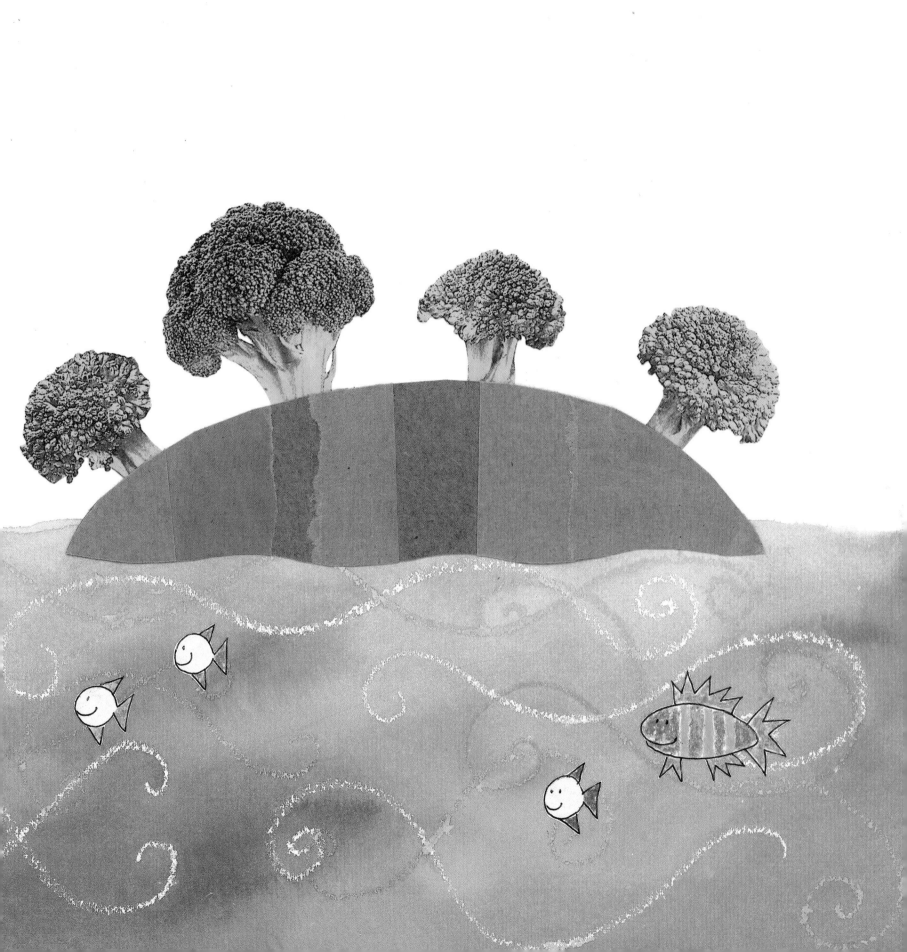

Where was he?
Oliver heard a loud noise.

Gurgle,
gurgle,
gurgle.

"Hello?" called Oliver. "I'm Oliver."

"Hello, Oliver!" said a penguin.
"Do you want to come aboard?"

Oliver climbed up the ladder.
The gurgle, gurgle, gurgle sound grew louder.
It came from all the penguins slurping their drinks.

"We're on vacation," said the penguin.
"We can do what we want all the time. So we slurp our drinks and we fly around for fun."
"Penguins can't fly," said Oliver. "It takes more than just wings, you know."

"We have jet packs,"
said the penguin.
"Do you want to try?"

It was the best fun ever.

Then the sky started to turn orange.

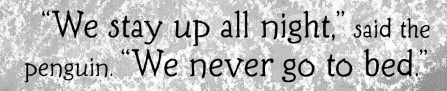

"We stay up all night," said the penguin. "We never go to bed."

Oliver thought about that.

"My mom will miss me," he said.
"And I don't know how to get home."

"We'll help you," said the penguin.

Oliver climbed back
into his submarine.

"Hold on tight," said the penguin.

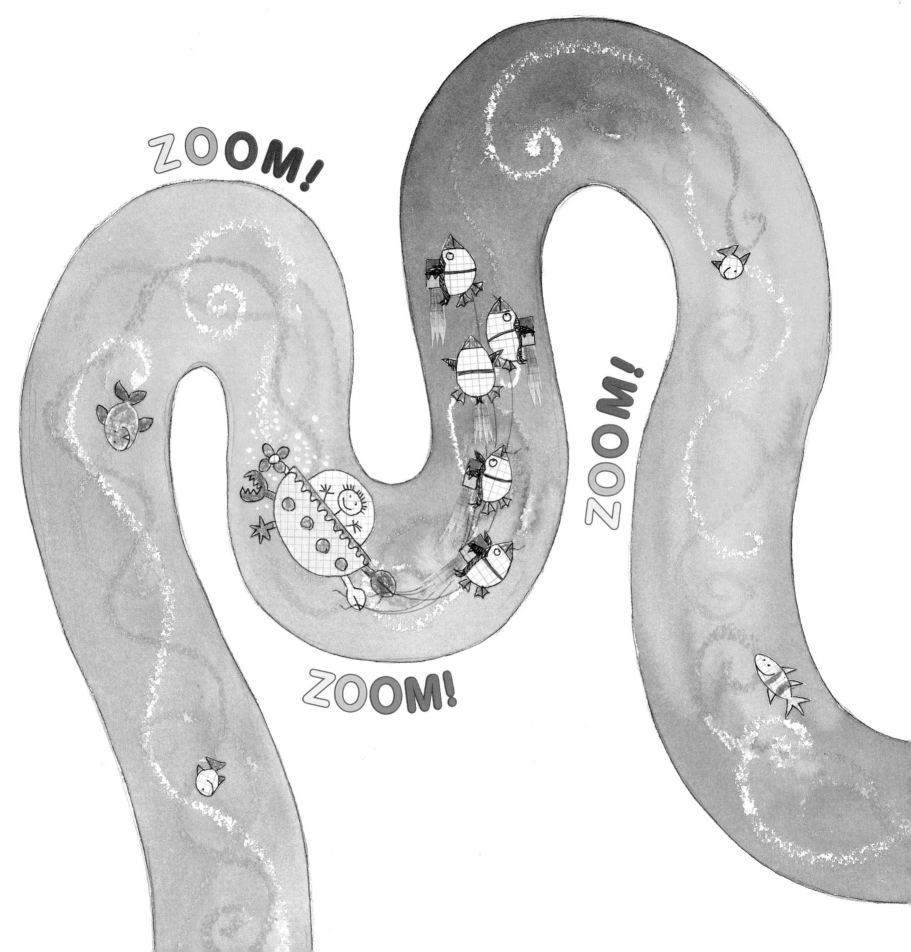

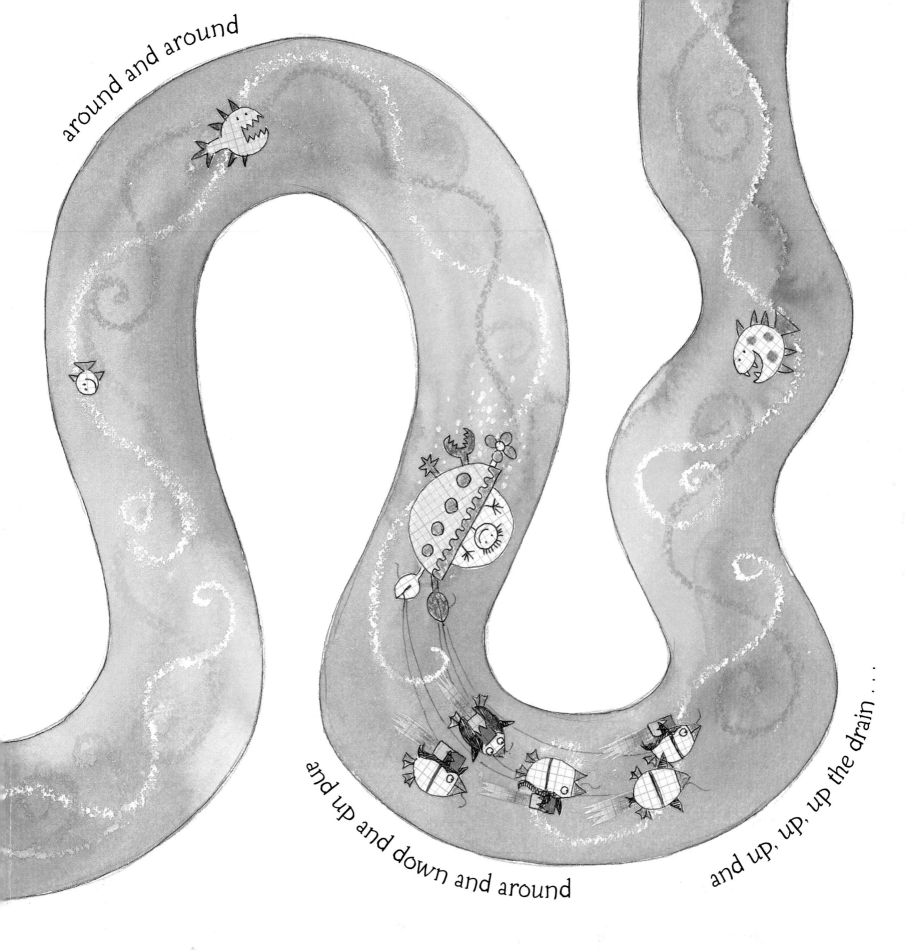

around and around

and up and down and around

and up, up, up the drain . . .

"Oliver!" called Mom. "Just in time for dinner."

"I went down the drain," said Oliver.

"I missed you," said Mom.

"I know," said Oliver. "That's why I came back.

"Tomorrow, I'm going to build a jet pack."